MW00935698

The author firmly and openly acknowledges all copyrights, licenses, and trademarks of all musicians/bands used as pop culture references in this novel.

Readers, this is a complete work of fiction. Any character in this novel that you feel resembles someone you know is entirely coincidental. It is set in the very real town of North Berwick, Scotland, and surrounding areas. While I have done research to make the setting as realistic as possible, any errors of detail or fact are solely mine, and for those possibilities I apologize in advance.

Dedication

For Mary, who fell in love with Angus first.

My friend, my sidekick, "My Gertie"—may our antics continue until we're old and in the nursing home where we'll terrorize the staff with an inflatable alligator.

Author's Acknowledgements

I'm so blessed to have so many talented people surround me on this writing journey. They all know who they are, but I feel that you all should also know who they are. *Snaring Angus* exists because of them. I certainly couldn't have done it alone.

Cover photo by Siberius Photography. Beautiful work!!

Many thanks to Michelle and Jo for being my guinea pigs... I mean, beta readers. Thank heavens you both feel comfortable enough with pointing out my mistakes!

Natalie and Amanda—you girls are my social media angels! You gals are the hardest working PAs a writer can ask for. I am so not worthy.

Friends and family who always ask "How's the writing?" You keep me going when it all feels a bit too much. Please keep asking so I'll keep going.

snare: one of the more common drums in marching bands and drumlines, and the primary drum of a drumset. Known for powerful, staccato sound.

snare: something by which one is entangled; something deceptively attractive.

Chapter One

Kerry Hunter stood outside The Ship's Inn Tavern. It was only four-thirty in the afternoon, but she was already completely exhausted. Now, she faced another eight or nine hours on her feet before she could even think about stopping for a rest. Her shoulders drooped as she pulled open the door. *Please, don't be here. Please, don't be here.*

As she entered the pub, she automatically glanced over at the stage area and squelched an exasperated groan. She'd been dreading this all day. She had just put her bag behind the bar and was tying on an apron when it started—her continual battle.

"Jesus, Kerry. You look like bloody hell."

She figured she did. It was the height of tourist season, and she'd run herself ragged over at Harbor Point Manor cleaning rooms before coming in for her shift at the pub. She just didn't need Angus-bleeding-Donaghue telling her so. As she walked to the swinging double doors leading to the kitchen, she lifted her head, looked over, and put a sweet smile on her face.

"Angus?" She batted her lashes, "Choke on those damn drumsticks." Shooting daggers with a narrowed gaze at his smug face, she wearily propelled herself through the swinging door.

William Holmes turned and glared at his mate. "Why are you so mean? You know she's had to pick up extra jobs to help pay her mother's bills. She's worn out! You," he jabbed a finger in Angus' face, "are an arse."

Angus regarded William as he continued to get the equipment set up for their set tonight. The lad was the youngest of The Captain's Folly, only in his mid-twenties and played keyboard for their pub band. The dreamer of the group. He was like a nerdy younger brother. Their other two mates, Brett who sang vocals, and Malcolm who played guitar and frequently went by the nickname Mack the Knife or simply Mack, were the oldest of the group, both in their late thirties. Angus closed the generation gap of the foursome, and despite their ages, the four men had grown up together as friends. When Brett opened his pub, they took advantage of the open venue to show off their musical skills every weekend for the locals. Though it annoyed him to admit it, William was right. Once again.

Yeah, he supposed he appeared mean. Hell, he was mean—with Kerry at any rate. They'd always battled back and forth for as long as he could remember. They just pushed each other's buttons. He'd actually almost felt sorry for her when she came dragging in for her shift. The bags under her eyes had looked fairly black against the light violet of her irises, and the lengths of her black hair were coming undone from a hastily roped ponytail. He knew weary when he saw it and figured she'd be dead on her feet before the first set of the night started if she didn't have some encouragement. The only way he knew to do that—throw it in her face. He knew she'd gather up what little energy she had left to throw insults back at him. He'd never thrown one at her yet where she didn't give back as good as she got. Truth be told, he wouldn't have paid her any mind, but you throw in the fact that she was dealing with her terminally ill mum... well, a man had to have some sympathy. Even with those that annoyed you to your wits' end.

***

She was on her way back to the kitchen to pick up another food order, when a large hand grabbed her arm and stopped her.

"Have you eaten yet?"

She blew her hair out of her face and looked up at her boss, and owner of The Ship's Inn Tavern, Bretton Keith. He'd barked out the question and was now looking at her expectantly.

"No time yet. It's crazy in here tonight."

Grabbing the tray from her hand, he pushed her over to the bar.

"Donald, let Kerry borrow your seat for a while."

The gray-haired gentleman got up swiftly for someone in his late sixties and relinquished his chair with a flourish.

"Happy to do it. Take a seat, lass; I know you're worn clean off yer feet." Donald patted Kerry's shoulder sympathetically.

As Brett walked off, he called out to his bartender. "David, go grab her a plate of something."

Alan, Donald's ever-present and equally aging side-kick, leaned around so he could look at Kerry. "Tell us, love, how's your mother doing?"

Kerry let out a sigh and gave the two pub regulars a sad smile. "About the same, really. Of course, she tries to let on like she's getting better."

"Well, you know our offer still stands. Anything at all, you call us." Alan offered.

"Thanks, Alan...Donald," she nodded as David placed fish and chips in front of her. She'd just begun to eat when she heard an annoyingly familiar rumble of Scottish burr behind her.

"Lady of leisure now, are we? My, my. If only the rest of us could be so lucky. What *is* your secret, Duchess Hunter?"

Kerry glared up at the mirror that ran the length of the bar on the facing wall. Angus stood behind her, smug and arrogant as ever. He'd been running his hand through his dark, shaggy hair, so it was a bit in disarray, that right eyebrow raised in an ironic lift. *I think he's cocked that damn eyebrow so much it's permanently stuck that way, the moron.* He was sporting a very thin bit of scruffy beard these days, which somehow actually managed to make him look more conceited than usual. His icy blue eyes watched her in the mirror. Arranging her face into a look of disgusted disdain, she fired back.

"Yes, for the next five minutes I am. If you actually had any friends yourself, you might experience the same." Returning her attention to the food in front of her, she threw out off-handedly, "What's with the beard, anyway? Thinking of joining a commune?"

"See, Kerry, that just proves there's something off with you. All the other ladies think it's rather dashing." He gave her a smirk as he ran his hand down his jaw, eyes teasing.

"Ladies? Oh, is that what the street-walkers are called these days? I didn't know," she sniffed.

Alan and Donald broke out laughing at her snub.

"Stop while you're ahead of yourself, lad," Donald advised.

"Ay, let the poor lass eat in peace," Alan followed.

Angus walked off laughing, leaving Kerry to fume in silence. Donald and Alan were still chuckling beside her. Rolling her eyes, she looked over at them. "If I'd had any sense at all, I'd have found a way to drown him when we were in primary school."

Both men burst into loud laughter at her statement as she carried her plate back to the kitchen and returned to work.

Chapter Two

Kerry pushed her housekeeping cart down the hall and let herself into room ten. The guests had just checked out, leaving her an hour to get the room ready for the next check-in. She crossed the room and threw open the drapes to let in the sun and stood there staring out at the choppy waters of the Firth of Forth stretching out in front of her. She could tell the wind was up by the whitecaps on the waves. She wished she could stand there staring forever, but she had to finish this room so she could take her mum to the oncologist. Whisking the sheets off the bed in one huge yanking motion, she threw them in her cart, retrieved the fresh sheets, and remade the bed. Forty-five minutes later, the floors were hoovered, the bathroom cleaned and resupplied, and the main room tidied. She rolled her shoulders to relieve the tension in her neck as she wheeled her cart back to the storage closet. She was about to finish locking the door when she heard someone behind her.

"I take it room ten is ready. You certainly are efficient, Kerry."

She turned at the sound of the friendly voice to find the elegant Eleanor Blackwood smiling at her. Fortunately for Kerry, the owner of Harbor Point Manor had agreed to take her on as a maid when her mum fell sick. Eleanor was flexible with her schedule as much as possible to accommodate Kerry's need to be at her mother's many medical appointments. Between the hotel, the pub, and her primary job as a columnist and blogger for the local paper, she was able to keep their heads above water. Barely.

"Thanks. I'm playing beat the clock today, I'm afraid. Mum has another appointment," she replied, blowing her bangs out of her face and tossing her hair back.

"I hope all goes well. You let me know if either of you need anything."

The sympathy in Eleanor's kind eyes was sincere as she reached out a hand and briefly, but warmly, clasped Kerry's wrist. It was in moments like this that Kerry found she came the closest to losing her grip on her strength. What she wouldn't do to give in and lean on someone else for even just a little while. To let someone else carry this ever growing mountain of struggle a few miles. The very idea felt like nirvana at the moment, but she just didn't have that luxury. She knew that if she ever let her guard slip, let herself cave under the worry and fear, she may never scrape together enough strength to stand back up and carry on again. And that was the last thing her mum needed right now. She straightened her shoulders, managing to hide her wince at the twinge in her back. "We're okay. But thank you." With a quick smile and a nod, she headed for downstairs.

***

They'd been sitting in the waiting room for what felt like hours. Kerry glanced at the large wall clock opposite them. They'd been there twenty-five minutes. There seemed to be no sign that they'd be called back anytime soon. *Might as well get some work done.*

She pulled out her laptop and powered it on when her mother leaned over.

"You can take a little break, love. You're working too hard."

"Don't worry, mum. I can knock this out before we even get called back." Kerry didn't look up from the screen as she typed out a blog post for the paper on the trends for this year's tourist season. Luckily for her, the extra work at the hotel and pub provided quite a bit of insight into this particular topic. She finished off the six-hundred word post, hit save, and packed up the laptop.

"See? All done!" She grinned over at her mother. Alice Hunter had always been a fair slip of a lady. Blonde hair, pale complexion, and light blue eyes. These days, her hair was thinner and a dull ash, her skin ghost-like, and eyes that flitted between red-rimmed and watery, depending on the day. Knowing her mother was sick and seeing it felt like two entirely different things to Kerry. If mum looked fine, then she could almost ignore what was happening and forget that there was some ugly mutant cellular mass slowly destroying her. Seeing her now, weary and pained, made the knowledge of what was happening so much more real.

"Hunter?"

Kerry looked up at the nurse that stood in the doorway. *Well, here we go.* She gathered her things and stood up with her mother. They crossed the floor and followed the nurse down to a small conference room. They both sat on one side of the table.

"Dr. Brody will be with you shortly."

The nurse left quickly, the click of the door snapping into the jam deafening in the silent room. Kerry jiggled her right thigh up and down under the table, but the movements were so tense and controlled that it was almost imperceptible.

"Why do doctors make you wait forever?"

"Just be patient, Kerry. Don't wish your life away."

Kerry stopped breathing for a moment. "Mum," she whispered as she shook her head. Looking over at her mother, she wished she could take it back. She would sit at this table for twenty years waiting for Dr. Brody to walk in if it meant her mother would be there with her.

Her mother just smiled at her. "I know, but you have got to stop having such an impatient temper."

"I'm patient when I have to be."

"When are you ever patient, love? I know you." Alice shook her head and laughed quietly. "I don't know who on earth will ever put up with you."

"Who says I need putting up with?" For all her mother's efforts, Kerry had so far managed to avoid any serious romantic entanglements.

"Mrs. Hunter?" Dr. Brody walked in, all aloof professionalism, as is the way with doctors. The man sat down across from them and placed a file on the table in front of him.

"Good afternoon, Dr. Brody." Alice gave him a friendly nod.

Kerry watched as he opened the file and stared at the pages in front of him. From where she was sitting, it just looked like a jumble of numbers, statistics, and long-winded, unpronounceable words. As he cleared his throat, she started bouncing her leg a little harder under the table.

"We have the preliminary results from the experimental treatment."

"How did it go?" Kerry asked all in one rushed breath.

Dr. Brody flipped over the top sheet of paper and rubbed his chin. "Yes, well unfortunately, we're not seeing the results that we hoped we might."

"I see." Alice reached over and placed her hand on Kerry's arm.

"We had hoped that the tumor would have reduced by fifty percent with this new treatment, but the tests are currently only showing only a very minimal decrease of less than one percent. The cancer is simply not responding."

The doctor turned over another two sheets of paper and paused a moment. Clasping his hands in front of him, he looked both women in the eye, first Kerry, then Alice where his gaze remained.

"To complicate these initials tests, your white blood count has accelerated at an alarming rate. We believe all the indicators are present...the disease is starting to spread."

Kerry looked over at her mother. Alice sat there, calm and collected, while Kerry felt like she was coming unglued at the seams.

"How long?"

"Mrs. Hunter, of course we can only give you our best guess, but I think we're looking at somewhere between two and three months given the placement of the primary tumor."

Kerry flinched as if someone had struck her. Hot tears filled her eyes.

"If that's truly where we are Dr. Brody, I believe I'd like to cease treatments. Unless you feel they may help."

"At this point, they may give you an extra week, possibly two. I can't say that they'll improve your quality of life at this point, so that is a consideration."

"I think we'll just let nature go its own way, then." Alice offered the man a sad smile.

"I won't make you continue your appointments; however, if you need me, you call me. Would you like me to make hospice care arrangements for you?"

"Must that be done today?"

"No. We'll make the referral call this week and set up the first visit for next week."

The women sat quietly as Dr. Brody gathered his file and stood.

"I wish the news had been more positive. Call my office anytime should you need anything over the coming weeks. Feel free to use the room as long as you need. There's no rush." He turned towards the door, then looked back, his face full of sympathy. "I'm so very sorry, Mrs. Hunter."

"I'm—" Alice cleared her throat and tried again to speak. "I'm very grateful for all your efforts, Doctor. Thank you."

Dr. Brody nodded of his head before leaving the room.

Kerry clung to the hand on her arm and stared at Alice, completely stricken.

"My God, mum. I...I..." Kerry found she couldn't finish speaking. The tears that had been pooling in her eyes finally spilled over.

"Don't cry, love." Alice gently wiped the tears from Kerry's face. "It'll all turn out as it should."

They left the surgery and ventured back home, Alice completely spent in the passenger seat. Kerry let her mother rest and kept silent. She was spiraling in a whirlpool of emotions as it was. Kerry really didn't think she could manage a conversation right now, and she certainly didn't think she could offer any comfort to her mother. She stared ahead, willing her eyes to stay dry. They passed the village center of North Berwick and turned off towards the harbor point. As Kerry finished the turn, there was a muted pop, and the car suddenly dropped on one side.

"Bollocks!"

Kerry struggled to get the car off of the road. Pounding the steering wheel, she turned off the ignition. She dropped her head to her chest and inhaled deeply, trying not to completely lose it in front of Alice. "I'll be back, mum."

She got out of the car and regarded the tire at the rear. Flat as a bleeding shortbread. She purposefully did not ask the "What else can go wrong?" query because after today she knew what that would be, and she absolutely wasn't ready for that. Would never be ready.

Kerry jerked the jack and wrench from the boot and placed them beside the tire. She walked up to her mother's door and opened it a fraction. "It's completely flat. Are you okay in here while I try to change it? I'll have to lift the car on that side, but you should be fine."

"Don't worry about me, love."

Kerry started to walk back when she heard her mother again. "Besides, you can just wait."

She stepped back up to the door. "What do you mean wait? We can't sit on the side of the road all evening. You're exhausted." Although, now that Kerry was looking at her mother again, she seemed to have gotten the slightest tinge of color back in her cheeks.

"Oh, we won't be sitting here. It's all handled, Kerry," Alice assured with a hint of a smile.

Kerry's mind was racing. How on earth could her mother have done anything in the span of forty-five seconds? Then it hit her like a tidal wave. She immediately let out a long, exasperated groan. "Mum! You didn't!"

"I most certainly did. You don't need to tackle that tire by yourself, and besides, that's his job. I don't know why on earth you have such a reversion to him."

"Because he's the spawn of Satan, mum."

"Kerry Elizabeth! Don't say things like that..."

Kerry heard her mother's voice trail off as she stalked over to the doomed tire. She hastily whipped her hair into a sloppy bun with a hair tie and grabbed the jack. If she hurried maybe she could get the tire changed and back on the road before he got there. She positioned the jack under the car and started to crank the handle to lift the tire off the road.

"Do you even know what you're doing?"

Her hand slipped and dropped the crank at the sound of Angus behind her. Her spine stiffened out of sheer reflex. She'd been so focused on trying to get done before he got there that she didn't even hear him come up. Buying herself some time, she stood up slowly, wiping her hands on her jeans. *This is the last thing I need today.*

"We're just fine here. You can carry yourself back to the bog you crawled out of."

"Oh, that's not what your mother thinks. As she's the one tha called, she's the one I'll be listening to."

She stepped up to him. "You really don't—"

Angus firmly gripped both arms, picked Kerry up a full fiv inches off the ground, pivoted, and set her down two feet awa from the car. She was so stunned that in the thirty seconds she stood there alternating between trying to stammer out her outrage and gaping at him like a fish, he'd knelt down by the car and started twisting that crank at double the pace she had, raising the back of the car swiftly off the pavement.

Well, there was no getting out of it now. Best to just let him get on with it. She could still feel the pressure of his harsh grip on her upper arms. No one had ever lifted her off the ground like that. Kerry was trim, but she was solid; she was certainly no delicate waif. Who knew Satan's spawn was so strong?

Angus stretched over to grab the tire he'd brought with him. Kerry tilted her head as she took in the view in front of her. *What do you know? Satan's spawn has a very nice—.* She lifted an eyebrow, then immediately frowned. *I can NOT start his ridiculous eyebrow thing! Get a hold of yourself, you silly girl!*

She quickly turned away and stared off down the street. It was all the stress of this afternoon. That was it. That was why she had suddenly and completely lost her mind. The sooner he was gone, the sooner she could get herself back to normal...well, as normal as you could get when trying to wrap your head around the fact that the person you've relied on your whole life was about to disappear from it forever. Goosebumps broke out over her arms and her neck in the cooling air of the evening. Anticipating being home long before now, she hadn't thought to bring a coat with her. She wrapped her arms around herself to try and stay a little warmer as she listened to the clink and clang of metal tools hitting the pavement or crashing into and onto each other as Angus worked just behind her.

Kerry felt as though her shoulders were just two huge knots holding her head up. She rolled her head from side to side to try to loosen the tension. These days she constantly felt like one huge walking ache. If she felt like this, she couldn't begin to imagine what her mother must be feeling like. As that thought brought tears to her eyes, she immediately willed them away. Pity parties could wait. Her mother couldn't.

"Oy! You're ready."

Kerry whipped around to see her car sitting level on the pavement, all the tools stowed away, the boot closed, and the flat tire hanging from Angus' left hand. She glanced from the tire to Angus and shrugged a shoulder. "Right. Thanks."

She was going to walk back to the car, but something in his gaze stopped her. "What?"

"Nothing. Just—nothing. Are...you okay?"

Either she was delirious or he actually appeared to be slightly concerned. She couldn't figure it out. She surely wasn't going to stand here in the street and tell him all her woes. She refused to deal with it herself just yet, and there was no way she would talk to Satan's spawn about it. "Sure. Fine."

He hesitated a moment, then shifted the weight of the tire in his hand. "Right." He shook his head and walked around to say a few words to her mother.

As Kerry opened her door to get in, he raised his head and locked eyes with hers. She thought for a moment he was going to say something else, but he just smiled back down at her mother and closed the door. He was walking back to his truck when he called out a simple "See ye, Kerry."

She watched him drive away before sliding into the car. As she turned the key, it struck her that this was the first time they'd ended a meeting without throwing parting barbs at each other.

Chapter Three

Kerry let out a relieved sigh as she walked out of her bedroom. Mum had finally had one of her rare good days and was resting comfortably in front of the telly. Sarah Collier, the American who had moved to their little village and was now dating her boss, had called her and insisted that she fix herself up and come down to the pub as a customer, not a worker. She'd struck up a friendship with Kerry during her time working in the pub. As this would be the first night off she could remember in about four months, it really hadn't taken much arm-twisting to get Kerry to agree.

"Mum? Are you absolutely sure you don't need me to stay with you?" Kerry walked up to her mother's chair and fussed with the blanket thrown across her legs.

"Will you stop fussing? I'm fine. You need a night to relax and have a bit of fun, love. You worry too much." Alice smiled up at her, eyes crinkling in the corners with joy. "You look lovely. You'll be breaking hearts tonight."

"Ach, Mum," she rolled her eyes and tossed her long curls behind her shoulder. "The last thing I need."

"No, that's *just* what you need—and don't roll your eyes at me." Alice's face shifted into that warning glare perfected by mothers the world over.

Kerry stared down at her for a long moment, a habit built from years of dueling wills between mother and daughter. Then, she abruptly stuck out her tongue, pursed her lips and blew an air-kiss.

Alice's laughter filled the room. She had known how their dueling always ended, with humor and affection. "Have fun, darling. You deserve it."

Kerry fought the lump in her throat and a sudden seize of panic at leaving her mother by herself. Yet, with the sound of her mother's laughter in her ears, she couldn't bear to disappoint her by staying. That laugh had been pretty absent lately. If Kerry didn't know better, she'd have thought it was her mum going out for a grand time at the pub rather than herself. She slung her little bag over her shoulder and waggled her fingers in a wave. "I won't be gone long."

"Don't you dare come back here before eleven!"

"Okay, okay. Fine. 11:05," Kerry laughed as she closed the door.

Fifteen minutes later found her entering the pub with a smile on her face. The door had only just closed behind her when a familiar American accent caught her attention.

"Over here, Kerry! I've saved you a seat with me."

She walked up and grinned at Sarah. "I hope you've cleared this with my boss. I can't afford to get on his bad side."

"Oh, don't you worry about that. He knows you need a night off, and I do have some influence on him when I really want to use it."

Kerry held up a hand. "I don't want to know the details of *how* you convinced him. I'll simply say thank you." She perched herself up on the barstool. "What are you drinking?"

"It's a Scotch night."

"Oh good!" She leaned up and yelled down the bar. "David! Get me a round of whiskey."

"You got it, babe."

Seconds later a glass with a healthy pour of Scotch appeared before her. She snatched it up and turned to Sarah. "Well, here's to a night off!"

"Absolutely," Sarah replied as she knocked her glass against Kerry's. "How's your mom?"

"She's had a good day today. She told me not to show my face again before eleven," she laughed.

"Who's your friend, Sarah?"

Kerry managed not to cringe at the sound of Angus' deep voice behind her. She was also barely keeping a rein on the fist she wanted to connect with his face as she slowly turned on her barstool to face him. "Why does Bret keep you around again? Donald's three-year-old grandson is a better drummer than you are."

"What's with the get-up, Ker? Local vampire coven have a rummage sale?"

Kerry couldn't explain why, but on impulse, she responded with the only way she'd found to shut Angus up. She looked up at him with a smirk on her face, lifted her hand, and, very deliberately, bit her thumb. Three seconds passed, and she saw his nostrils flare slightly right before he stalked off to his drum set, muttering profanities to himself. Her face broke into a grin as she knocked back the rest of her whiskey.

If he ever clapped eyes on old Mrs. McDougall again, he was gonna kill her (if she was still alive, that is). It was all her fault anyway. Angus kept up his silent string of obscenity as he stomped up to the stage and started yanking on equipment for the evening. He'd almost forgotten about the whole *I bite my thumb at you* nonsense, but leave it to Kerry to bring it back when he least expected it. When they were teenagers, the two of them had been stuck in the same literature class, studying *Romeo and Juliet* with old lady McDougall. As soon as Kerry had learned that *Master Shakespeare* had used the gesture as an insult, she'd immediately taken to employing that as her favorite comment to his verbal digs. The trouble was that it ended their battles all right—by making Angus very uncomfortable. Despite her flippancy, that one simple action had never failed to somehow turn him on. The latter years of his youth were spent in a very frustrated confusion of aversion and attraction for Kerry. When they got older, she'd dropped the habit, returning him to his comfortable status quo of mere irritation and snarkiness.

Until tonight. He had no idea why she'd done it, and it was certainly the last thing he'd expected. He hadn't recognized her sitting there with her back to the door. All he had noticed at first were long, black curls and legs encased in black leather that seemed to go on forever. The shock of it being Kerry when she faced him hit him full force. She had on a filmy little white shirt that skimmed her curves and some kind of purple and grey stuff around her eyes that made them look even larger and more violet than they usually did. He'd resorted to his standard quip, and just when he was gearing up for one of her stinging retorts, she had placed her thumb between her full lips and scraped her teeth along the pad. He was a grown man, and she had managed to make his heart start racing and his mind go blank in that one instant. The fact that she was able to do that pissed him off. He'd had some fantasies about her after she started that thumb business when they were in school, which he'd never revealed to anyone—ever. He hadn't had those in years, but they all came flooding back one after the other, only with a very grown-up Kerry.

This was going to be a long night.

***

Two hours and several drinks later, Kerry and Sarah were still talking and laughing. The band finished their set and made their way over to the bar.

"Hey, Angus! Seem to be a little off your rhythm tonight." Kerry tilted her eyes up at Angus and let out a throaty, sarcastic laugh.

She could see him winding up to snap back at her. Then, suddenly, he stepped closer to her, and the expression on his face smoothly shifted from a snarl to a very sexy smirk.

"Tell me, Kerry," he taunted confidently in a low voice, "just what do you really know about my rhythm."

Kerry didn't know if it was the whiskey or the way he was looking at her or if she was having a stroke, but she found that her ears were buzzing and her tongue was tied.

"I...we-well...you..."

"That's what I thought," he scoffed. Snagging a full pint glass from the bar, Angus started to walk away. "Still can't hold your liquor, can ye Ker?"

Kerry stared after him, brows furrowed in frustration. Of course, *now* she could think of a quick retort. But why had her wit suddenly failed her just then? She'd seen him throw that same look at other girls in the pub before, but he'd never actually used it on her. They had a very firmly delineated relationship built on mutual hatred and revulsion. It worked. She lifted her glass in a fit of annoyance, only to find it empty when she tilted it up.

"So why are you and Angus always sniping at each other?" Sarah asked as she propped an elbow up on the bar.

Kerry swung her head to look at her friend. "Habit."

"Habit? Really?"

"Yeah. We've been at each other's throats practically from birth."

"Uh huh." Sarah lifted an eyebrow in disbelief. "If you say so."

"What?"

"Nothing, nothing." Sarah motioned for David to bring another round and laughed quietly to herself.

The night was waning thin, and the girls were still having a grand time even though the pub had emptied of customers several minutes ago. Kerry couldn't remember the last time she'd laughed so much. It had certainly been way too long, and she tried not to pay too much attention to the small nagging pinch of guilt in the back of her mind for enjoying herself.

"Oh, come on Wills!" Sarah entreated playfully. "Please do it! Just one time."

William frowned at the pair from down the bar. "No. I refuse to humiliate myself."

"No one's going to yank away your man-card," Sarah countered.

Kerry walked over to sweet, loveable William and looked up at him with pleading eyes. "I may not have this much fun again for a while. Don't be mean to a girl who's having a hard time." Fluttering her lashes at him and smiling sweetly, she was the picture of the sympathetic coquette.

"Oy, don't fall for that guilt trip, mate," Angus snarked as he saw his friend starting to cave. "I can't take that tonight." He grumbled to himself something about a headache.

William reluctantly gave in, grudgingly. He was the youngest of the group with a sensitive soul. Knowing what Kerry was going through, he just couldn't find it in his heart to turn her down. "Fine. But only one verse and chorus, and that's it."

Bret laughed from behind the bar. "Now, we're in for it." He grinned as he watched Angus roll his eyes.

"Oh brother."

William walked up to the keyboard and started a quick intro to the well-known song. Kerry and Sarah stood away from the bar and began dancing as they sang the first verse of ABBA's "Dancing Queen".

Mack looked on from his barstool with an insolent look on his face, and as the girls started shouting the chorus out at the top of their lungs, Angus just leaned forward and beat his head against the bartop. He hated this song, and their screeching didn't help it any.

Bret simply laughed. "It could always be worse, Angus."

"How on earth could it possibly be worse than this?" Angus simply slammed his head to the oak bartop and groaned loudly.

The girls finished their song, and William walked away from the keyboard.

"You two owe me for that."

Sarah and Kerry surrounded the young man in a big hug. "You know we love you, Wills!"

"Are you done squawking for the night, Kerry? You completely managed to make Sarah sound like some kind of banshee, and she, unlike you, can actually sing very well."

"Just shut it, Angus." Kerry moved away from William and stomped over to get right in Angus' face. She tilted her head back to look up at him as they stood toe to toe. "Shut. It." She weaved almost imperceptibly on her feet.

"Make me," he challenged, low and sharp, his gaze unwavering.

"Okay, that's it! Everybody go home. I'm done," Bret ground out as he walked around the bar to pull Angus away from Kerry.

Kerry and Sarah laughed as they gathered their bags. Mack leaned over closer to Angus. "You should take her home, mate. She doesn't need to walk back by herself."

"Is that so, Malcolm Lennox? Then you can take her home. Besides, what on earth would happen to her on the point? Nothing ever happens in this village, you know that."

"'Ave you never stopped to think that the reason you two knock heads all the time is because there's something between you two?"

"What?" Angus stared at his older friend as if he had just sprouted wings and started flying around the pub. He'd never heard anything more ridiculous.

"Stop being an idiot. You've got feelings for her, and what's more you know it deep down. Always have." Mack crossed his arms, daring Angus to deny it.

"Oy, now who's being the idiot." Angus left him standing there as he walked away.

"Takes one to know one, mate." Mack said to his friend's retreating back.

As Angus walked towards the door, he looked over at Sarah. "Make sure she gets home. She's likely to fall into the Firth in her state."

"I'm NOT drunk!" Kerry shouted as he yanked open the door and stalked out into the night. "I. hate. him," she spat.

Sarah threw her arm around Kerry's shoulders and grinned. "No. You don't."

Kerry did a quick double-take at Sarah. "No, I do."

"Come on, I'll take you home," Sarah suggested good-naturedly.

The girls walked out of the pub together, but Kerry stepped away from Sarah. "Thanks for the offer, but I'm good. I promise."

"Are you sure? I don't mind."

Kerry could see a slight hint of worry on Sarah's face. Although she hated to be the cause of that, she had to admit that it felt good to know her concern. She felt so isolated from everyone of late, and this bit of connection was just what she'd needed.

"Absolutely. It's dead quiet, and I'm not far." Kerry tilted her head with a smirk. "Besides, I'm already in trouble with the boss for taking tonight off. I can't also be responsible for him having to wait around for his sweetheart to come home."

Sarah chuckled. “True enough.” She threw up her hands in surrender. “Just be careful. We’ll see you tomorrow.”

“That you will.” She watched as Sarah started to turn back to the pub. “And hey...” She paused for a moment as her friend looked back over her shoulder. “...thanks for tonight. I needed it.”

“Anytime. I had a blast.”

Kerry waited until Sarah had gone back into the pub to join Bret before turning for home. The fresh, chill air quickly cleared her head as she walked down the village streets to home. Quiet, dark, and still. A sleepy little village resting by the sea.

Chapter Four

Angus was elbow-deep in the underpinning of a lorry, tackling a broken axle. The fact that he hadn't been able to get Mack's last words to him at the pub the other night out of his head had only served to put him in a foul mood. He was just twisting a wrench around the gear cover when the words flooded back again. "*You have feelings for her, and what's more you know it...*" His hand slipped, and he scraped his knuckles, dropping the wrench with a clatter. "Bloody hell!"

"All right there, lad?"

He rolled out from under the lorry and swiped his bloody hand against his pants. He glanced up at his father who was looming over him. "Aren't you supposed to be with mum today?" He regarded his father sardonically.

Craig Donaghue had turned over his auto-repair business to his son two years ago, but he still found reasons to swing by several times a week. Angus always figured it was because he really wasn't ready to sit at home. His dad always had to be doing something. It was one of the many traits they shared, along with sarcastic wit, unforgettable blue eyes, and a trim physique.

"I can only take so much chattering about gardens until me ears start bleeding, son. Had to plan an escape," his father laughed.

"Well, you can escape yourself under this hunk and fix this blasted axle, old man."

"Oh no! That's why you run the shop now. I'm too old to be working under big pieces of machinery these days."

"Oy, just who d'ye think you're trying to fool? You didn't retire because you were getting fat and lazy."

"No, just lazy. That was reason enough." The two men laughed.

As their laughter died off, his father got serious. "So you never answered me earlier. You all right?"

Angus recognized the deeper tone and excessive rolling r's of his father's voice that clearly indicated he was worried. For as long as he could remember, when his father was bothered or concerned, somehow his burr became even deeper and thicker. His accent, like the worry, seemed to come from a deeper level of his soul. Craig Donaghue wasn't an emotional man by any means, but that change in his voice always struck a chord with Angus.

He narrowed his eyes and looked away from his father. "Ay, fine," he muttered offhandedly. He had barely kept himself from scuffing his shoe along the ground like he used to do when he was little. Why was it that no matter how old you got, your old man could still make you feel like you were eight years old?

"You're not a wee lad anymore, son. If there's something bothering you, you can talk to your ol' dad, you know."

Angus felt his father's strong, warm hand clap him across the top of his shoulder. The grip of it was sure, steady, and a comfort. Angus exhaled deeply and felt his body relax as his shoulders dropped, easing the tension in his neck. He returned his gaze to the man in front of him. Two pairs of clear blue eyes regarded each other seriously. One set concerned, the other set...resigned.

"Don't know what to tell you, Da, except you don't really need to worry."

"Always worry, lad. That's my job, even if I am retired." Craig Donaghue cracked a smile, trying to help lighten the mood. "Just don't seem yerself is all. Could it be a spot of trouble of the feminine variety?" At that brilliant stroke of detective work, Craig crossed his arms in front of his chest and leaned back entirely pleased with himself for possibly nailing down his son's predicament.

"What? I. No. No trouble with the ladies. When have I ever had trouble with the girls?" He crossed his arms, mirroring his father.

"You stammered there, lad. No, you've never had problems getting the lasses. You've just had trouble keeping them is all."

He couldn't believe what his father was saying. He knew it had been a bad idea to try and pretend that there wasn't anything on his mind. The fact that his father had so unknowingly hit the nail on the head was not helping to improve his mood, however.

"Who's to say I want one to stick around long-term, anyway?" He countered, leaning back against the lorry that hovered a couple feet off the concrete floor on a hydraulic lift. His face was carefully schooled into a cynical smirk.

Craig watched his son for a long moment. He knew he'd hit a nerve. He also knew he wasn't likely to get Angus to talk anytime soon. Better to let it lie for now.

"Fine. I won't push ye. Just yet."

Angus peeled away from the lorry and walked closer. His expression softened now that he knew his dad wasn't going to make him discuss things he wasn't even sure of. "Thanks, Da."

"Ye have nae heard from your sister, 'ave ye?"

"Not recently, no." Seeing the worry in his dad's eyes, he quickly added, "Ach, you know Blair, Da. She's likely trekking up some mountain, as like, and won't have mobile service."

"Right ye are, lad. We'll see you this week for supper, ay?"

"Ay."

Angus watched as his father walked out of the shop before turning back to the blasted lorry. One momentary victory down, one to go. It was either him or that bleeding axle. Snatching up his forgotten wrench, he climbed back under the vehicle.

Chapter Five

Angus was sitting behind the kit, pounding out a very heavy syncopation, building a crescendo on the symbol as Sarah hit the transition to the final chorus on a new song they were performing for the pub. It was a crowded Saturday night. Beyond the regulars, there were dozens of tourists out for some local color on their seaside holiday—although the "local color" had become a little more international of late. Sarah was laying on a thicker American accent than she normally had, but he had to admit it really worked with the song. He eyed his pal Brett, and sure enough, he was eating up her performance. His mate was far gone, and no mistaking it either, having fallen for the auburn-haired history professor a year ago. After she'd gotten his attention by singing for him in the pub once, he'd added her to a couple songs in their set each week.

A bead of sweat rolled down his temple, and he rolled his shoulder in aggravation since he couldn't reach up and swipe it away. Scanning the tables, he locked onto Kerry. She'd just dropped off a round of pints and was crossing back over to the bar. She stuck her tongue out at him as she passed below the stage. He didn't miss a beat on the snare as he slowly winked back at her. He had to bite back a laugh when she stopped in her tracks befor wrinkling her nose in confusion and making her way back to th bar.

As they finished the song to close out the set, Mack steppe over to Angus as he set down his guitar.

"What's in yer head, mate?"

"Not a thing, Mack." Angus finally took his sleeve and swiped at the sweat on his temple.

"Oh yes, there is. Written all over your ugly face." Mack continued to study his friend for a long moment. He leaned forward conspiratorially. "You've been thinking about what I said." He grinned slowly and slyly. "Ay, that's it. Watch yourself, Angus."

"Oy! Don't preach to me, old man." Angus crossed his arms over his chest.

"Not lecturing you, mate. Just saying watch out for her. Now's not the time to be playing games."

Angus dropped his defensive pose. Mack was right. As much fun as it would be, he knew better than to go but so far with Kerry given all she was facing. "No intention of that, Mack. Besides, we'd end up killing each other in the end. Not worth the hassle."

Mack watched Angus, then shook his head. This made two of his mates entangled in love and that was enough to give Mack serious anxiety. Avoiding the "l-word" was the only way to stay safe. "Am I the only one that still has any sense left at all?" He walked off the stage, leaving Angus by himself.

As Kerry crossed the floor again, Angus walked to the edge of the stage. She was coming back with a tray of empties when he stopped her.

"How about getting a man a drink, Ker?"

Kerry stopped and looked around. "Oh, is there one nearby? I wasn't sure."

He stepped closer. "Just look in front of ye."

She tossed her long ponytail. "You? Please. See if your friends will grab you one. I'm busy."

She carted the tray of empties over to David. Angus watched as she spoke something to the bartender and then headed for the door. He hesitated only a few seconds.

Kerry had rounded the corner of the building and leaned back against the brick wall. She closed her eyes and concentrated on clearing her head of the noise and the clatter. She never used to take breaks, especially when the pub was busy, but since that last doctor appointment, she'd started taking ten minutes to herself when she got wound up or felt as if she were about to fall off her last leg. It wasn't much, yet the few moments of solitude seemed to help her get herself back in focus. Even if it was only for the next couple of hours. She really didn't know how else to keep going, so she now simply took her days in two-hour chunks. Get through this two hours, then worry about the next two. It may not be the best way to deal, but it was her way.

"Slacking on the job, I see."

Her eyes popped open. She silently screamed her frustration. Wasn't there anyone else he could bother? She rolled her eyes as she turned her head slightly to look over at him. She didn't move away from the wall.

"I'm entitled to a break."

Angus stepped a little closer. "Haven't you ever wondered?"

"Wondered what? How many times you were dropped as a baby? When aliens from Planet Zoron were coming to take you back to the colony? Why you breathe?"

He stepped even closer and leaned his shoulder against the wall. He smirked at her responses. Typical.

"Why we fight so much?" he said lowly. "Why we *like* to fight with each other?"

He was only inches away from her, and it was making her uncomfortable. This was so not the program. What was he getting at?

"Because you're a bloody moron!"

"Oh yeah?"

The crazy idiot was just smiling at her.

"Absolutely! You've been the bane of my existence since we were four years old! You're the most aggravating—"

Angus abruptly stopped her tirade by capturing her mouth in a kiss. Kerry immediately went still at the contact. It was as if all the nerve endings in her brain short-circuited and blew out. She could feel his lips curve in a smile as he broke the brief kiss and pulled away. Everything had been at warp speed and in slow-motion all at the same time, and Kerry swayed from the disorientation.

"Uh-huh." He turned and started walking away.

She stood there watching him walk around the corner of the building when her brain kicked back to life. She took off after him.

"You wait just a bloody minute, you demon from hell! I'm not through with you yet!" She rounded the corner and saw him just a few feet away. He had stopped when he heard her calling after him.

"Let's have it then, you harpy!"

He stood there grinning at her. He should be locked up in an insane asylum.

She stalked toward him, jabbing her index finger at him with every step. "You're off your rocker, ye are. Why haven't you been locked up yet? What on earth do ye think you're getting at anyway? And why, for the love of all that's holy, did you just do that? We had a thing. You yell and poke fun at me, and I insult you. The thing worked. It's worked for our whole lives, and now you decide you want to mess with it. Angus Donaghue, you drive me to the brink of utter distraction!"

She had been him giving the business the entire time it took her to stride up to where he was, and he'd only grinned wider at her. She could tell he wasn't paying her any attention, which just infuriated her even more. She took one last large step to put herself toe to toe with him. She tilted her head to look up at him and grabbed his shirt with both hands.

"You make me want to kill you," she stated simply before yanking his shirt to draw him closer. Standing on her toes, she kissed him. Unlike before, when he'd kept a little distance between them, she felt Angus wrap his arms around her and pull her up against him. The contradiction between the solid, firm arms holding her against the hard wall of his chest and the soft pressure of his lips had her free-falling. She loosened her grip on his shirt in order to wind her arms around his neck as he angled his head for another, deeper kiss.

Just when his hands flexed to grip her more firmly, she broke the kiss and stepped out of his arms. She remained rooted there, wide-eyed and shaking her head at him.

"That...is so not good," she whispered in apprehension. She took off running for the door to the pub.

Alone, in the dark, he called after her. "I thought it was pretty great!"

Chapter Six

Kerry had managed to finish making the bed when her mobile buzzed in her pocket. She absent-mindedly reached for it as she walked over to her housekeeping cart. Swiping at the screen, she saw the notification:

Can't stop thinking about that kiss.

Kerry stared up at the ceiling. She knew for a fact she'd never given Angus her number. She let out a huff of annoyance.

How in hell did you get this number?

Your mother.

Well, erase it!

What if I don't want to?

I could make you.

It'd be interesting to see you try.

Some people actually work for a living. You're wasting my time.

I work for a living...it's just dirtier. ;)

Yes, I'm sure you're very familiar with working in squalor.

Still thinking about that kiss...

Ignoring you.

Kerry jammed her mobile back in her pocket and slammed he cart towards the door. She was having a hard enough time trying not to think about that kiss, and now he was texting her about t. It had been two days, and she could still feel his warm breath n her lips. Running her hands through her hair, she tried to clear he vivid memory from her mind unsuccessfully.

***

Six hours, ten cleaned hotel rooms, two blog posts and this week's community column submitted to her editor, Kerry wiped down the bar with a cloth while keeping a discreet eye on Angus. He was in conversation with Donald and Allen at the other end of the bar. He had just run his hand through his shaggy hair.

"What are we staring at?" Sarah interjected rather loudly.

Okay, so it hadn't been *that* discreet an eye after all. Kerry immediately started polishing the bar as if she could rub a hole in the varnish. "Nothing!"

"Come on," her friend pleaded as she leaned up over the bar. "Angus got you fixated finally," she whispered conspiratorially.

"Him? Ye're full of it!"

"Oh no. I don't think so."

"You're nice enough for a Yank, but I still say ye're off your bleeding rocker!" Kerry turned away to fill a pint and hand the glass over the bartop to the waiting customer.

"Your boss doesn't think so," Sarah countered.

"He's the biggest lunatic this side of Edinburgh. Well, excepting Lord of the Jesters down there," Kerry jerked her head sideways to point at Angus down the bar who was laughing his foo head off at something the two old geezers had said.

"Careful, Kerry." Sarah smiled. "*Methinks the lady doth protes too much.*"

Kerry laughed. "You're just giddy with love and think every one else must be as well."

"Maybe. Don't knock it til you try it, as they say."

"Don't knock what?" Bret's deep voice broke in as he wrapped his arms around Sarah from behind.

Sarah leaned back into him and turned her head to smile at him. "Love."

"True." He looked over at Kerry with a smirk. "And just who is it you're supposed to be in love with then?"

"Her? She's too mean to love anybody!" Angus scoffed as he came closer to the three of them.

What! "I don't see a line of women falling all over you, Donaghue."

Angus caught the bar rag Kerry threw at him and leaned in. "Don't need a line o' women. Just need one. If she's the right one." He handed the rag back to Kerry, and as she grabbed it, she felt him slide one finger down the inside of her wrist under the cloth as he pulled away. For that brief instant his face was set in a serious expression, his eyes searching hers.

"But who am I to deny the banquet until then!" He stepped back and threw Bret a cocky grin.

Annnnd, the arse is back. Bloody, stupid man! Kerry threw her hands on her hips. "Ye're a bleedin' lech!"

Angus turned that grin to Kerry, and it reached the sexy slant of his eyebrow. "Don't you wish you knew, Duchess Hunter." He walked off laughing as Kerry stood there fuming.

"Sack him!" She glared hotly at Bret.

"He doesn't work for me, love," Bret laughed.

"Then sack me!" Kerry stalked off to work out her frustration on some tables that needed bussing, Bret and Sarah's loud laughter following her across the pub.

Customers were gone, and Bret was emptying the till. David had already left, so Kerry was making sure everything was ready to lock up. She called out a goodbye to Mack and William as they walked out.

"I'll check the kitchen, Kerry," Bret called behind her.

She was lifting a chair and turning it onto the table as two hands grabbed her exposed waist.

"When are you giving us another kiss then, Ker?"

"Never!" She spat out even as she shivered from the feel of his low voice rumbling in her ear and the warm pressure of his hands resting on her sides.

"Never's an awful long time, love," he whispered against her cheek. She could tell he was smiling without even turning her head to look at him.

She hesitated only a moment and then threw her elbow back, jabbing him swiftly in the gut. She heard him let out a huffy groan as he jerked his hands away and stepped back. She pivoted to face him. "We're not doing this...whatever this is."

"Why no—"

"Haven't you finished with her for tonight, mate? Leave her be! You two are worse than old dragons, snapping and blowing fire at each other," Bret called from the kitchen door.

Angus threw his hands up. "I'm going." He backed away and then walked out of the pub.

Kerry crossed over to the bar to grab her purse. "Why are you and he mates again?"

"He makes me laugh, and he's a good bloke." Bret regarded Kerry thoughtfully. "Despite your prejudiced opinions."

"If you say so," she capitulated. Slinging her bag over her shoulder, she made for the door. "See ye, boss."

"See ye!"

Kerry walked out of the pub and automatically turned left to head for home. She was just walking blindly when a shadow stepped away from the wall of the building into her path.

"Angus!"

"You know, I believe I'd like the sound of you calling out my name if you didn't put so much hate behind it."

"That's because I loathe you. Don't you have some kind of home to go to?"

"It'll keep. I'm more interested in exploring what's really going on here, Ker."

"Nothing. Nothing is going on here."

He took a couple steps closer, and she backed up. He stepped forward again. "Come on, Kerry. You can't tell me you really believe that."

"I can at that."

"Look me in the eye and say it, then." His voice was gruff with frustration, and he leaned down into her space. Kerry looked up at him, at war with herself.

"Ye can't! You can't look me in the eye and say there's nothing here," he challenged.

Blast it! Kerry threw up her head and glared at him. "No. Satisfied?"

She skirted around him to walk on, but he snagged her arm and pulled her back. Angus ran his hands along her jaw and into her hair to trap her. He dropped his forehead to hers. "Why are we fighting it then?" His question was barely more than a breath, he'd spoken so lowly.

Angus sensed the moment she gave in. Her shoulders sagged, and he heard her take in a ragged breath. The resignation in the sound of that breath ate away at him. He stood there frozen, unsure of how to fix things.

"Because that's all I know to do...fight. Been fighting all my life."

Flashes of Kerry's life flickered swiftly through his mind. She didn't have to explain it to him. He knew. Her showing up to school when her dad ran off after her sixth birthday. The two of them spouting insults at each other at age ten in the school yard...fifteen and in English class...eighteen and on the village street with a group of friends. Kerry working at the paper while working her way through university. Her mum getting sick. It was how she handled what life dealt her—like a warrior.

"You know you don't have to fight me too. Let's not anymore." He moved his hands away in order to pull her into an embrace, but he felt her withdrawal.

"I can't deal with this, Angus."

"Don't walk away from this, Ker. Come on," he pleaded.

"I have to."

He watched the glint form in her eye. In a series of fluid motions, the weary warrior pulled her armor back on. He watched her as she straightened her spine. Righted the bag on her shoulder. Jammed her hands into her pockets. Curt nod of the head.

"I have to," she asserted. "And you'll be needing to let this drop."

"Kerry—" He reached out, but she was already striding away from him. He was left standing once again in the dark, alone.

"Now, what in bloody hell do I do?"

Chapter Seven

The two months Dr. Brody projected had turned into three, and to Kerry's amazement, her mother was still hanging on despite being so weak. When the doctor had confirmed that Alice likely only had days left, Kerry had taken time off from the pub and manor to stay home with her mother. It was just fortunate that the paper let her work mostly from home anyway, given the nature of her job. She didn't have to be in an office to write her posts and columns. She'd barely left her mother's side for the last two days.

Settling onto the side of the bed with a cup of tea, Kerry watched her mother's breathing become more and more shallow. Alice had been listless and weak for days. As much as she wasn't ready, she knew her mother was simply tired. She leaned forward and touched her mother's arm. "Can I get you anything, Mum?"

Alice gave a soft shake of her head. "No, love. You don't have to worry about me," she assured in a thin whisper.

Kerry leaned forward. "If you say so," she laughed quietly, her vision blurring with tears.

"I do say so. I'm your mother." Alice smiled weakly and stuck the tip of her tongue out at Kerry just like always.

Kerry let out a brief laugh as Alice closed her eyes and released a long breath. The air in the room went completely still. The ticking of the clock on the wall the only sound. Kerry's heart shattered into jagged pieces as her sweet and feisty mother finally gave up the fight.

Angus shivered in his coat as the wind blew in off the cold waters of the Firth of Forth. The small group had come here together after the quiet and simple service at the church. He watched her standing by the Firth, just out of reach of the waves. Sarah stood close to her with Bret, Angus, Mack, and William standing with him, behind them. This part was just for her. Just for her and her mother. None of them were eager to do this, but she'd asked them. As hard as it would be, particularly for him and William as they rarely sang, all four of them would sing for her and for Alice.

"Are ye ready, Kerry?" Bret asked quietly.

Kerry could only nod in response. Angus knew she wouldn't speak because she would completely go to pieces. The four of them looked at each other, and when Bret gave a soft nod, they started singing, soft and low. Angus kept his eyes on Kerry, noticing when she stiffened her back to keep from falling apart as their voices swirled around her in bittersweet melody. She stepped forward into the lapping water and opened the lid of the small urn she carried. As she tilted it, the ashes filtered out into the water of the Firth, the wind catching some in the air and drawing them out towards the sea. Beside him, William's voice choked up. Inhaling deeply and quickly before the song's next words, he clapped a strong and comforting hand on his young friend's shoulder.

As the last notes of their song drifted off on the air, Kerry turned back faced to face them. Mack gave a low cough in his throat as William quickly brushed a stray tear from his eye. Bret rubbed Sarah's arm in comfort as she sniffled into a tissue. Angus suppressed another shiver as he watched Kerry's long, black waves whip around her head in the wind as she walked towards them.

"Thank you. That's all I can get out right now, but thank you." She nodded in gratitude to the little group of friends. Her tired eyes rested on Angus.

"You come on over to the pub when you're ready this evening. We'll have a little gathering," Bret encouraged as he gave her a hug and patted her shoulder.

"I'll be by after a while." Kerry nodded again, accepting a kiss on the cheek from Sarah.

Mack and William started back up the beach, with Bret and Sarah behind. Kerry turned back to face the waves as everyone started to head back. She stood there, just watching the movement of the Firth.

Angus remained, keeping an eye on Kerry. She seemed lost, but then, he could only imagine that's exactly how he'd feel if he'd just lost his mother. She had yet to shed a tear that he knew of, and that worried him. It wasn't natural to keep grief bottled up. He studied her for several long moments. As she crossed her arms in front of her and started to curl into herself against the cold, he silently moved forward and draped his coat over her shoulders.

"Thought you'd left with the others."

Angus shook his head at the terseness of her voice. "I'm not leaving you out here by yourself."

"I don't need babysitting, Donaghue."

"Ay, you're a grown woman. Doesn't mean you can't accept a little support."

She wheeled around to face him. "You are not using today as your in with me."

Angus stared down into her stormy violet eyes. "I know you think I'm an arse most days, and I'll likely agree with you on that fact. But if you really think I'd use the day you lay your mother to rest to take advantage of you, then you've got a colder heart than I'd ever give you credit for." He hadn't yelled. He hadn't snarled. He'd simply and quietly rebuffed her typical knee-jerk reaction. When she continued to glare at him in silence, he turned and strode away.

"You forgot your coat!"

Angus halted and dropped his head in frustration. He hesitated, finally lifting his head and walking on. If he turned back to her, he was like as not to throttle her in her stubbornness. He couldn't do that out of respect to Alice's memory. Though God, and likely Alice Hunter, knew he desperately wanted to. And, just as likely, figured she probably deserved it.

Chapter Eight

Kerry was dragging one foot in front of the other. It was another double shift day—one at the hotel and then another at the pub. How much sleep had she gotten this week? Four hours...five? She had no idea, but however many it was, it wasn't enough. She wouldn't hear any objections to her going back to work just after the funeral, but after months of sprinting between three jobs, looking after her mother and losing her, she was really reaching the end of her rope. Fridays were always busy at the pub as everyone put the work week behind them, so naturally she was running non-stop.

She had paused behind the bar to pull a few pints for a table and catch her breath. The Captain's Folly had been playing for a while, and to close out the first set, Sarah was singing a slow, bluesy number, full of soulful sadness. It was a new number so the noise had dimmed a bit as folks were taking in the song.

Kerry had dropped off the pints and returned with a tray of dirty glasses for the washer. Her back was to the room, and the constant weariness she'd been carrying for so long finally broke under the weight of melancholy lyrics and Mack's rhythmic guitar chords. Tears of fatigue and frustration slipped from her eyes before she even realized they'd begun to pool. Throwing her head back, she let her shoulders drop and let out one deep burst of breath before swiping away the tears and willing her eyes to dry.

As the song finished, she put the rest of the glasses in the wash and rung up a couple tabs for tables ready to leave.

"Running dry back here, Ker. How long does it take to run a tab?"

She looked up to find Angus taunting her with an empty whiskey glass. Mack had been the only one on stage with Sarah for that last number. Stomping over, she snatched the glass from his hand, and never taking her eyes off his, she grabbed a whiskey bottle on her left, poured exactly two fingers of the light amber liquid, and shoved the glass back at him across the bar. Receipts in hand, she left him standing there to deliver the checks to the waiting customers. He won that round, and she'd let him. She didn't have the fight left to even throw out a half-assed attempt at insulting him. She just didn't care anymore. Why the hell did they go at one another like they did anyway? It took so much energy, and she was out of that these days. If it stoked his ego, then so be it. As far as she was concerned, she had just surrendered the battle of wits.

Angus stood there staring after Kerry as she circled tables, tending to the customers. He'd planned to egg her on more than he had, but when she'd lifted her violet eyes to look at him, he had stopped at what he saw reflected in them. They'd been wet with unshed tears, and what little light she'd had left in them was completely gone. He knew she tried to hide how exhausted and worried she was most of the time, but in that moment, any pretense she'd been clinging to had been worn away.

Even now, she smiled and pandered to the customers, but he saw the tightness in her smile. He noticed the circles under her eyes and the brittleness of her laugh. Normally, he got a kick out of messing with her because he was always curious about what she'd throw back at him. But just then, for the first time, he regretted throwing the little barb at her, and he wasn't exactly sure how to deal with that. Eyeing that shot of scotch wryly, he whisked it off the bar and quickly downed it.

He rushed over and grabbed her elbow after she dropped the last ticket off and propelled her towards the door.

"Angus Donaghue, you let go of me!"

Kerry tried to yank her elbow away, but he had a tight grip on it and wasn't letting go. Angus steered her out of the pub and walked them around the corner of the building and out to the bit of shore by the waters of the Firth. Away from the street, the night surrounding them was black and frigid. He could feel the goosebumps break out over his arms. Only when they were a few feet away from the edge of the waters did he stop walking. Letting go of her elbow, he stood back two paces and waved his arms up and down in front of her. "Right then. Have at it, Ker."

"What's in your head, Angus?"

She was confused and defensive; he could hear it in her voice "Whatever that was back there in the pub."

"I don't know what you're talking about you moron."

"Oy! Ye're not fooling me, ye know." He stepped forward an leaned into her space, putting his face right in front of hers. " know you."

"You know nothing! You have no bloody idea about what I'r going through! Get out of my face." Angus felt her try to shov him away from her but braced his feet so she couldn't move him

"Fine! You won't move, I will!" She turned to walk away, bu Angus grabbed her wrist to stop her.

"I do know what you're going through. I haven't experienced it myself, but I see the hurt eating away at you."

Kerry let out a hard sob and tried to pull away. When that didn't work, she turned her body back to face Angus and threw a punch at his shoulder. He caught her fist with his free hand and pulled her closer to him.

"You can cry out here. Scream. Curse me all the bloody way into next week. No one to see ye, and I can take it."

"No," she choked out on another sob.

He let go of her wrists and wrapped his arms around her and hugged her tightly. "It's not weakness to grieve, Kerry," he encouraged. In a lower voice, he whispered in her ear, "You can fall apart for a while. Right here. Right now. I've got you."

She was furiously shaking her head against his chest when Angus felt the first warm tears soak through his shirt. He instinctively flexed one arm around her tighter and moved his other so that he could cradle her head with his hand, fingers curling into the lengths of her midnight hair. She had surrendered the fight with herself when he felt her go limp in his arms, and she began to sob.

He stared up at the dark sky above them. He'd been so wrong—he couldn't handle her grief. Her sobs cut like knives against his ears, and his cold shirt was clinging to him uncomfortably, soaked with her tears. He wanted so badly to make it stop, but was completely powerless. She needed this release though, and he knew it. No matter how hard it was for her to give into, or how awful it was for him to watch.

Angus felt her clutching at his shirt, and when her body sank under the weight of her sobs, he felt the collar cut into the back his neck. He'd never felt so helpless or so isolated in his entire life as standing there on the deserted shore, surrounded by darkness and taking on an ocean of grief.

Kerry didn't know how long she'd been crying, but she felt cold down to her bones and her limbs felt extremely heavy. She was just so tired. And mortified. She tripped a bit over her feet as she tried to back away from Angus's embrace.

"I...I have to get back," she stammered between sobs.

"You're not in any shape to go back. Come on," he steered her away from the water. "I'll take you home." He pulled his phone out and sent off a quick text to Bret to let him know Kerry wasn't fit to finish her shift.

Kerry pulled back and stopped. "I really don't think I can go home right now. I just...can't," she admitted lowly.

He put an arm around her and kept her walking. "Right. Then I'll take you to mine."

They walked on two more steps before he added, "Bet you never thought I'd say that to you."

She sniffled and quietly sobbed the whole walk to his flat. She tried to stem it, but she found that the dam of emotion had broken, and there was no putting it together again. Her steps were heavy and dragging, and by the time they walked the last half a block, Angus was practically carrying her, holding her up with one arm. She leaned into him, wanting to ignore how good it felt to have someone to lean on.

She let him lead her into his home and settle her on the brown leather couch. It suited him. Simple, no-nonsense. All the creature comforts a single guy requires with no extra fuss or frills. She found herself laughing quietly to herself.

"What's so funny?" He handed her a bottle of water.

She sighed with a tired, but amused, smirk on her face. "Always figured you were a slob, Donaghue."

"My mother did not raise a slob. Drink some of that," he demanded.

"Bossy, bossy, bossy!"

"Yes. Now, bloody do it." He stared down at her, arms crossed over his chest.

He watched her take several long swigs of the water and then moved across the room. "I'll be right back. Don't go anywhere."

Kerry finished the bottle of water and was settled into the corner of the sofa when he came back in the room.

"You changed your shirt," she observed as he sat down beside her.

"Well, the other one was slightly damp." He gave her a sympathetic smile.

Kerry shut her eyes and groaned. She opened them again to find his icy blue eyes watching her. "I'm so sorry. I never imagined I could cry so much. It's rather embarrassing."

"Why? You're bloody human, Kerry."

She found she couldn't look at him. Those eyes. Seas of blue that were always full of sarcasm, irony, laughter, conceit. Any of that she could take. What she couldn't take was staring into icy depths that now held fathoms of unspoken emotion. It was unnerving—like looking into a mirror but not recognizing the reflection.

She felt him shift beside her, then his cool hands on her face.

"Look at me."

She gave a huff of resignation before looking at him.

"I know you better than anyone else. If you can't be vulnerable around anyone else, you can with me. I admit that in the past my powers were seemingly used for evil," he conceded with a sad smile, "but if you ever noticed, I never let anyone else get away with that. I teased you—"

"Mercilessly."

Angus chuckled. "Mercilessly. But never maliciously."

"Could've fooled me."

"Never maliciously. I only wanted your attention, and I got it," he grinned widely, stroking his thumb along her jaw. His expression softened. "I think I've loved you my whole life."

"You can't possibly think that!"

"I can think that. I *know* that. I've loved every part of you—your fight, your heart, your mind—all my life. Don't you see it?"

Kerry could only stare at him in blind panic. Love her? But...he hated her. She hated him! Didn't she? Her mind was spinning in a million directions, and in the midst of the whirling dervish of thoughts, she couldn't breathe because what he said was being answered over and over in her heart.

And that—was terrifying.

Kerry pulled away quickly, scrambling up from the couch in a clumsy hurry. "You don't mean that, Angus. You don't know what you're saying." She had backed across the room and was almost to the door by the time he stood up to stop her. She looked back at him, eyes wide with panic and shaking her head. Reaching behind her, she felt the cool metal of the door handle in her hand and as she slowly turned it, took one more step back. "I can't," she whispered before bolting out the door.

Chapter Nine

Two days later, and he still couldn't get Kerry to return his calls after she fled his flat in a panicked rush. Some profession of love that was. She couldn't get away from him fast enough. Maybe he really had read what was between them wrong, but he felt deep down that he was right. Unfortunately, he hadn't realized how hard it would be if she didn't feel the same.

It was late, and Angus sat at the small metal desk buried under stacks of paperwork. A greasy paper of fish and chips sat on top of one of the stacks. This was the part of the business he hated. Pushing all the damned paper. Give him a wrench in his hand and a rusty gearbox any day. His mobile started buzzing under the papers. Fumbling around for the phone with one hand, he snagged a chip with the other. He answered the call as he popped the still-hot chip in his mouth.

"Ay, wha—-ah!" He exclaimed, quickly huffing out rapid breaths while trying to chew the chip and cool the steaming heat at the same time.

"Hello to you too, big brother!" Blair laughed on the other end. "What are you *doing*?"

He blew out one last breath. "Eating a bloody hot chip, that what!"

"It's good to know some things still haven't changed," she retorted.

Angus let out a short, blasting laugh before turning serious. "How are ye? Where are ye?"

"Angus Donaghue, you sound just like Da! Since when did you start doing his *worried voice*?"

"I don't sound like Da!"

"Ah, you just did. It was weird."

"Well, next time don't take so bloody long to call!"

"Touche," she admitted. "I'm calling now, so you can all rest easy. How is everyone?"

Angus leaned back in his chair and stretched his legs out under the desk. "Oh, everyone's just fine. Mum and Da have been worried about you. The lads are all doing good."

"How's Will?"

"The same. Why?"

"What? I can't ask about my best friend now?" Blair gave an exasperated gasp on her end of the call.

"Ay, ay. Just figured you'd call the kid or something yourself," Angus placated.

"Stop calling him 'the kid'. He's not a child," she chided.

"Ye're both children—"

"—and you're a grumpy old man!" Blair interjected.

"Well, if you're just going to be throwing insults at me, I'll hang up and get on with my night. Thank ye very much."

"Don't hang up," she pleaded cheerily.

"Right. So where in bloody hell are ye?" He broke off a piece of fish and started eating.

"Just wrapped up a trek in Kiev. The episode should be up soon. We're planning the next trip though. I'm thinking Bangladesh."

Angus frowned at the excitement in her voice. "Blair, that's not probably the safest place to go right now. They're in complete political upheaval. Can't you just go to some island in the Caribbean?"

"Ugh. I do plenty of tropical trips. I have to make sure there's variety on the blog. The cultural aspects alone will be phenomenal. You know I'll take precautions."

"Kiev is bad enough. The Ukraine isn't all that stable now either. Just please...think about what you're doing before you go to another dangerous location. How about the Alps? Or Loch Ness! People always love to hear about Nessie."

"You're not going to get me to come home. Besides, Da tries the Loch Ness trick every time I call."

"Bollocks."

"I can't talk much longer. Any other news?"

Angus played with a chip on the greased paper. Giving a sigh, he continued, "Ay. Alice Hunter died this past week."

"Oh, poor Kerry. I'll be sure to send her a message. She ok?"

"She wants everyone to *think* she's ok. I know she's not."

"That sounds like Kerry. You two still at each other's throats?"

Angus tilted his head back to look at the ceiling. How to answer that? They were...in more ways than one.

"Something you not wanting to be saying, Angus?"

"No."

There was a long silence between the siblings. Finally, Blair quietly broke it. "Be watching yourself, brother. While I say that for her sake, I'm also saying it just as much for yours."

Angus swallowed past a sudden lump in his throat. "Ay," he assured in a gruff whisper. Clearing his throat, he prepared to let her go. "Think about what you're doing. And for God's sake, be careful."

"I love you, big brother."

"I might just love you back, blondie."

Blair could hear the smile in his voice. "I miss you, big brother."

Angus chuckled lowly. "I might just miss you back," he answered warmly. "Now buggar off so I can finish my supper!"

He ended the call as Blair continued to laugh. Grabbing the last chunk of the now cold, fried fish, he popped it in his mouth as he threw away the greased paper. He swallowed, surveying the papers in front of him. He felt the fatigue settle on him like a blanket and rolling his eyes, he groaned loud and long as he leaned forward and dropped his head on the desk.

Chapter Ten

It was Wednesday night, and the pub was fairly empty of customers. Kerry had rung the last of the tabs and was wiping down the bar when Bret called over the back of the large round booth.

"Come on over and join us." Bret waved her over.

Kerry dropped her rag and walked over to the crowded booth. She snagged a chair from the neighboring table and dropped into the seat. "You lot are nothing but trouble."

"Ay, but only the best kind," Mack winked at her from across the table.

Angus snorted ironically, but kept his opinion to himself.

"Well, I only know one kind of trouble..." Bret observed as he rose from the edge of the booth.

"Oy, what might that be?" Angus crossed his arms over his chest, a curious lift to his brow.

Bret turned to face Sarah and slowly dropped to one knee.

"No, you're not!" Kerry shrieked, slapping her hand across her mouth, her eyes wide with amazement.

"I think I have loved you ever since the first night you walked into my pub. I know I have loved you ever since the second night you walked into my pub and nearly choked to death on a shot of whisky."

Everyone around the table burst into laughter as Sarah gave a sigh. "Oh, Bret."

"Since you know my past, you know that I wouldn't ask this lightly. Mack told me from the beginning you were trouble. He was bloody right. But I can't think of a better way to spend the rest of my life...getting into trouble with you." He pulled something from his pocket and held out his hand to Sarah. Unfolding his fingers, she could see the antique diamond ring resting in his palm.

"Bret..." Sarah found she could only whisper his name as her eyes welled with tears.

He spoke again, softly, and his voice was rough with emotion. "This was my gran's. Promise you will. Promise you'll wear it and be with me for the rest of our days. I wouldn't want to spend it with anyone else."

No one moved as they all waited to hear her answer. They didn't have to wait long.

"Yes. Absolutely, yes."

Sarah brushed away tears with her free hand as Bret slipped the dainty vintage ring on her left. She let out a happy laugh as he leaned forward and kissed her.

"Bloody brilliant, mate!" William called out as he clapped Angus on the shoulder.

"What're ye pounding on me for? I'm not the one proposing!" Angus huffed out.

"Oh, loosen up, Angus! For a man in his prime, you're one mean ol' goat," William admonished.

Mack just looked on from the center of booth, trying, and failing, to ignore the pang in his heart. He pasted a smile on his face and addressed Bret. "I wish you luck, brother. Ye'll be needing it."

"Mack, you old softie!" Sarah teased, swinging around to stick her tongue out at him.

"Oy! Ker! Ye gone catatonic on us? You're face'll freeze like that...although that might be an improvement, come to think of it..." Angus smirked over at Kerry who still was wide-eyed with her hand covering her mouth.

Bret looked pointedly at Angus. "I'll not have you starting a fight with her on the night of my engagement! Leave her be!"

Kerry fumed silently at Angus briefly before running over and embracing Bret and Sarah. "I'm so happy for you! Slightly stunned, but brilliantly happy!"

On the walk home, Kerry reflected on Angus's attitude. Granted, it was the first time they'd seen each other since she'd fled from him the other night. His messages had sounded hurt and concerned, but he certainly seemed neither in the pub. However, she knew he was just "keeping up appearances". She hadn't been able to hide from his searching eyes all night. Eyes that were demanding answers.

She entered the dark, empty flat. She stood there in the silence, staring into the dark. She just felt so adrift. Walking to the first bedroom in the hall, she entered the room that was like a gaping hole in her life.

Kerry sat on the bed in her mother's darkened room. It was the first time she'd stepped foot in that room since her mum had died. She hadn't been able to bring herself to go through it until now. She didn't particularly want to deal with it at all. She didn't want to parse through the last things her mother ever touched. Head bowed, she reached her hand out and snapped on the porcelain lamp resting on the end table. Soft, white light illuminated the space, and Kerry stared at the simple green duvet for several, long moments.

Exhaling slowly, she swung her legs over the side of the bed and stood up. Kerry crossed the room to the closet. The next hour saw her dividing the contents into several piles. Items for the local charity shop, items she would keep, and items she would discard. She took her time, reliving memories with many of the items. Her mum's favorite ivory cardigan with the lost wooden toggle and fraying cuffs. The navy sheath dress she had worn to Kerry's graduation ceremony at university. A silk scarf boasting sunny yellow flowers. Humble and reliable garden wellies. The piles on the bed grew as the closet emptied.

She turned to the dresser across from the bed. The top was strewn with bits of costume jewelry, pill bottles, get well cards, lipstick tubes and perfume bottles. Leaning forward to collect the cards, Kerry noticed a long envelope addressed with her name. She knew the flowing, elegant script well. She fought tears as she sank down onto the bed behind her and slowly opened the letter.

Kerry, love—

There are so many things I wish I had the time to say to you. This certainly isn't how either of us figured things would turn out at this point. My only regret is that there is so much in your future that I'll miss out on. You are so talented, and I know that you're going to do so incredibly well in life.

The one thing I am worried about, Kerry, is how much you shut everyone out. I know, I know. You can say you don't do that all you like, but I'm your mother, and I know that you do. It's time for you to deal with that. Not all men are like your father, love. Please don't let his actions colour how you see everyone else. It's a very lonely life if you do. I don't want that for you.

You deserve happiness, and love, and family. I believe you can have all of that if you just hold out your hands and open yourself up. And while I'm sure some "spawns of Satan" exist somewhere, none of them are named Angus Donaghue. Don't fight him, love. The saying "thin line between love and hate" exists for a reason. Think about that...

I love you, darling girl. Be happy.

Chapter Eleven

Kerry had kept her distance all this time and wasn't sure how to undo it. Despite her constant protestations and denials, she knew Angus was right. There was something there, always had been, that drew them like the moon drew the tide on the Firth. They'd spent their entire lives fighting each other and fighting that connection. No matter how many years passed, that emotion didn't dissipate. It grew. Thoughts of him had kept her awake at night at times, wondering just what would happen if they called a cease-fire to their unending battle. She was so tired of fighting. Life was short, and hadn't she just had a large lesson in just how short it could be?

Unable to sleep, she ended up walking the point for hours in the dark and finally found herself standing outside his flat. It was late, gone past three in the morning. The entire harbor was asleep, the moon high above her head in a black midnight sky. The windows were all dark, and she knew he'd long since turned in, given the early start he'd have in the morning. Calling herself every kind of fool, she rapped her knuckles on the door several times.

The seconds felt like an eternity. No sound. She knocked again a little louder before shoving her hair back from her face.

"Oy! I'm coming!"

Her eyes welled with hot tears at the same time that she let out a laugh at his frustrated and gruff exclamation. She knocked again just to push his buttons a little more. The warrior couldn't quite completely let go of her fight.

"Do ye know what bloody hell time it is?"

She heard him shouting from the other side of the door, and she thought it'd never open. The need to see him pressed in on her chest, and the tears pooling in her eyes spilled over as the door suddenly flung open.

He stood there with thunder on his face from having been dragged from his bed. She drank him in with watery eyes. Mussed hair standing on end in several places. Grey lounge pants riding low on his hips, and that long, trim torso. Sweet heaven, but he looked like home.

"Kerry?"

The thunder faded from his face as she let out a half-laugh, half-sob.

"Time to surrender?"

She saw him jerk back in confusion for a long moment. She'd waited too late and missed her chance. Her mum had been right. She kept pushing until she'd completely pushed him away. Kerry felt her heart fracture and another tear tracked down her cheek.

She had dropped her head in preparation to leave when he hauled her against him. His kiss wasn't like the ones before. The testing, teasing ones. This kiss was one of longing and desperation and inevitability. His arms wound around her tightly, and she felt the corded muscles of his shoulders as she ran her hands over his warm skin and up into his hair. That slightly too long, shaggy hair of his. It felt thick and soft between her fingers.

He took the kiss deeper, and Kerry trailed one hand down his bare chest. She started to go light-headed and instinctively dropped her head back, gasping for air. Angus simply used that to his advantage to place long, open-mouthed kisses along her neck and collarbone. He snaked one arm up under her shirt to feel the soft skin along her spine as his other hand gripped her hip.

Angus felt the shudder of Kerry's ragged breath against his ear, and the sensation threatened to bring him to his knees. As his skin broke out in a fevered heat, he managed to hang on to one last thin thread of self-restraint. It physically hurt for him to lean away from her right now, but he didn't want to be some bad mistake one night in her life.

He took in the long, curling hair falling across her shoulder and her wide eyes. Her pupils were dilated, and he knew he'd give all he had to drown in those pools of violet if she'd only let him.

"Is this what you want? Truly what you want?" His voice came out strangled and low.

She reached up and took his face in her hands. "Yes. I'm not fighting anymore."

He wanted to believe that so much, but old habits were hard o break. And she'd persisted aggressively that she didn't want to ross this line. She'd fled from him so many times over the last ew months, and his heart didn't quite trust that she wouldn't flee gain now.

He tilted his head and stepped back warily. "Ye're not playing ricks on me now are ye, Duchess Hunter." He saw her wince at is statement.

She bit her lip as she shrugged her shoulders. She started to ach out to him, but stopped. "I'm not playing tricks. I'm not playing anything. You're right. You've been right all along. You're my touchstone, Angus. For every stage in my life, you've been there. Our communication has been twisted, and it's amazing we managed not to kill each other, but it's true. I can't imagine my life and you not in it."

She held out both arms at her sides, palms facing up. "The fighter comes to the enemy without weapons. Without armor. Without agenda. Only the knowledge that the enemy isn't really my enemy. Never was."

Angus stood there and took her in. Kerry, open and vulnerable for quite possibly the first time in her life. He thought she'd never been braver.

She cleared her throat, embarrassed. "I'd wave a white flag, but I don't have one."

Angus stepped closer and linked hands with hers, pulling her into him. "We don't need a white flag." He captured her mouth in a slow and intense kiss that went on forever. He heard the sof moan in her throat and finally broke the kiss to smirk lazily. "Let' see what you remember about my rhythm, then Duchess Hunter." He winked at her as he kicked out his foot to shove the doo closed.

"You just live to tease me, don't you?" She laughed lowly.

"You think I'm teasing?" Angus scraped his teeth across he earlobe as he pulled her hips tight against his. His voice was a lov hot breath in her ear as he continued, "I promise you I'm not teas ing. I can't think of a time when I've ever been more serious."

Kerry's head dropped back on a sigh, and he took full advan tage of the exposed lines of her throat. Slipping her jacket off h shoulders, he let it fall to the floor as he walked them back to h bedroom. They stopped at the foot of his tousled bed, and Kerry lifted her shirt over her head and let it drift out of her hand.

Angus knelt down to remove her shoes, and she could feel the heat from his hands through her pants as he ran them up the backs of her legs as he stood back up. That heat only intensified as his hands found the bare skin of her waist and up her spine to the clasp of her bra. That barrier removed, the feel of her skin against his was electric, and she wrapped her arms around him and scored her fingernails down the hard muscles of his back. The sound of his hissed breath at the contact made her feel strong and confident.

Just as she reveled in his reaction, he pivoted them in order to push her back and onto the bed. He captured her mouth in another open and passionate kiss as he let his hands explore her body. They lost themselves in a fevered haze as they finally surrendered to each other.

Angus blinked against the bright sunlight beaming through the window blinds. For a brief instant his heart clenched at the thought that last night was a dream, but the weight of Kerry's head on his chest brought him back to reality. She really was here. He closed his eyes again and exhaled a long, silent breath of relief.

"What's the matter?" Kerry's voice soft and slightly slurred with dreamy sleep.

Placing one arm behind his head, he smoothed his free hand down the lengths of her midnight waves. His chest rumbled with a suppressed chuckle. "Momentary panic?"

Kerry raised her head and studied his face, chin resting over his steady heartbeat. "Touche,'" she whispered, her face all sympathy and regret and hooded eyes that reflected deep purple whirlpools of emotion.

"I can't have you running away again. Can't keep watching you walk away anymore." His voice was deep and hoarse.

"That's why I ended up here. I feel like I'm drowning most of the time," she confessed quietly as she traced lazy circles on his shoulder. "I couldn't sit in that flat any longer last night and just started walking the point. I wandered around for hours, aimless. I didn't know where to go or what to do anymore. I just knew that wasn't home anymore, and I so desperately wanted to find that. I wasn't even thinking about where I was heading, but in the end, I walked up to your door and knew this was exactly where I needed to be."

"Ay, this is where you need to be, but why do *you* think so?"

She shifted so that her face was only a breath away from his. "You're my home, Angus."

It was merely a whisper, but that one whisper sounded like a thousand declarations in his ears. He wrapped his arms around her tightly and touched his lips to hers, softly and sweetly.

"That's the nicest thing you've ever said to me in my whole life," he said against her lips.

Kerry kissed him back. "Probably."

"I think I've figured out what all our fighting's been about."

Propping her elbow on his chest, she rested her chin between her thumb and index finger, watching him with one eyebrow skewed in an ironic smirk. "Oh yea? What might that be then?"

"Foreplay," he wickedly suggested with a smirk of his own.

They both stared at each other for a few seconds before bursting into laughter. Her head fell to his chest as she laughed, and Angus tightened his embrace, holding her for all he was worth while his body shook with laughter.

"Angus, I can't breathe!" Kerry's exclamation muffled against his chest.

He relaxed his arms and tilted his head so he could place a sound kiss on the crown of hers. "Sorry, love," the apology coming out between chuckles. He felt her still immediately. Christ, but he'd done it now.

She raised her head to look him in the eye. He saw her swallow hard as she tried to say what she was thinking. That momentary panic he'd mentioned threatened to kick back in. She lowered her lashes to hide her eyes, but then they lifted again to reveal tears. He felt his heart fracture a second time at the sight.

"Kerry..."

"I love you. I love your arrogance. I love your stupid eyebrow thing that you do. I love how you push me. I love your talent. I love your easy laugh. I love fighting with you. I love not fighting with you. You drive me crazy, and then you pull me back to sanity. I love you...just...you."

Angus couldn't speak for a long moment over the lump in his throat. He wasn't feeling very arrogant right now. This was quite possibly the most humble moment in his life, and he had no idea how he'd come to deserve it. Clearing his throat softly, he took a short, but deep, breath. "Marry me, Ker."

"What?"

He smiled at her surprise. "Well not today... but someday, and we'll go into the old folks' home when we're eighty, still snapping at each other like dragons." He wagged his eyebrows at her.

"I don't want to grow old still snapping like dragons!"

Angus shook his head, smugly. "You've already forgotten what I said. Remember, fighting is foreplay." He grinned at her, nodding his head.

"You are such a lech!"

"Only with you," he assured. "Come on then. Tell me you're not running away from me ever again," Angus pleaded. He leaned up and kissed her. "You're my home too, love."

"Yes, no more running," she breathed.

"YES!" Angus rolled Kerry underneath him and kissed her as if this were his last day on earth.

Chapter Twelve

Everyone had gathered at the pub this Monday night to have some time together without the pressure of having to wait on customers or play a set, as the pub was unofficially closed on Mondays. It had turned into somewhat of an impromptu engagement celebration for Bret and Sarah. Eleanor had even made time in her evening to leave her duties at her manor hotel and join them, and she was thrilled to celebrate the engagement of her good friend and the young woman who'd come to her hotel over a year ago on a solitary honeymoon after being jilted at the altar.

"I bet you had no idea this was going to be your story when you boarded that plane after your almost wedding," Eleanor teased.

"None! And I wouldn't have believed it if anyone had told me either," Sarah laughed.

"I wouldn't have believed *that* down there if I wasn't seeing it with my own eyes," Eleanor gestured discreetly to the couple sitting at the center of the bar.

"I knew it. Kerry was really quick to deny it, but I knew those two had something." Sarah looked down the bar and smiled widely.

Angus and Kerry had rather shocked everyone when they came in together earlier, arms wrapped around each other's waists. They shocked them even more when they announced they were finally giving in and were together.

"Hey, Angus? Does this mean we won't have to hear you two fighting all the time, now?" William leaned his elbow onto the bar top and looked over at his friend with a gleam in his sapphire eyes.

"No, ye ginger-headed pup," Angus replied sardonically. Turning his gaze to Kerry, his voice turned playful. "That's the fun part of this relationship!"

"Angus!" Kerry shrieked. "Shut up!"

He looked at his dark-haired beauty and gave her a cocky wink.

"I swear I will punch you in the throat," Kerry ground out, her voice dangerously low.

Angus leaned into her ear. "Keep on talking dirty, love."

Kerry stood up and looked Angus in the eye. She raised her hand and bit her thumb. As his gaze narrowed and grew heated, she laughed lowly and walked over to Sarah to chat.

William moved over to Kerry's vacant barstool. He looked at Angus, his face set in worry and seriousness. He ran a hand through his short red curls. "Angus, can't you talk some sense into your sister?"

Angus looked up. "What in bleedin' hell makes you think can get that girl to do anything she doesn't want to do?"

"I know."

"Besides, the only person she ever listens to is you. Can't understand why, but there it is."

"Not so much anymore. I'm down to just emails and postcards. She hasn't called in a while. Some best friend."

Angus studied the man beside him. "Ye know how she is, especially when she's prepping for a new trip. She'll just be busy is all."

"Sure. I just...," he shook his head. He couldn't tell her brother the bad feeling he was getting. Like something was off. "Never mind. Blair is Blair. I'll probably get a call next week at two in the morning from some corner of the world."

"Sure, mate. Don't worry." Angus gave him a brief pound on the back in reassurance.

Bret stood up from his seat and left Sarah talking with Kerry and Eleanor. Mack had remained apart from the group all evening, and Bret didn't want to put off what he had to say any longer. It was going to be bad enough as it was. As he walked past Angus and William deep in conversation, he reached out and smacked Angus on the back of the head.

"Oy! What's ye're issue!" Angus whipped around to glare at Bret.

Bret laughed and then looked at Angus intently. "Don't you buggar this."

Angus met his gaze, unwaivering, "No worries there, mate."

Bret nodded and then gave a wide grin before shaking his head and crossing the last few steps to reach Mack at the end of the bar.

"You find out ye got leprosy, man?" Bret sat on the stool beside Mack.

"Just minding myself. Problem with that?"

"No. Just figure you'd be wee bit more enthusiastic about my engagement, or at the very least with our company."

"You all say I'm the cynical old man in this group. Just playing my part, mate. You know I'm happy for ye. I don't understand ye, but I'll be happy for ye."

"Well, thanks," Bret drawled. "Look, been needing to tell ye something, so I'll just come right to it."

Mack turned his head to look at his friend. Bret's tone made him dread whatever he had to say.

Bret scrubbed his face with his hands, then looked Mack square in the eye. "Ye need to be knowing Ainsley's come back."

Mack's hand closed around his whiskey glass.

"Don't you throw that glass."

"I don't think I heard ye right." The hard knot in Mack's gut prayed he'd heard Bret wrong.

"Ainsley's come back to Edinburgh."

...the story continues in Bending Malcolm

Coming Soon

The story continues this summer with Bending Malcolm...

"What do you mean Ainsley's back?" Malcolm Lennox growled at his best mate, Bretton Keith as he slammed his whiskey glass onto the bar.

"Apparently, she moved to Edinburgh recently, and Sarah's gotten friendly with her. I couldn't believe it when she told me a few weeks ago." Bret shook his head and poured his mate another shot.

"A few weeks ago!" Malcolm shouted before lowering his voice to avoid attention. "You've known this for weeks, and you didn't think I needed to bloody know!" Steel-grey eyes shot daggers at the man in the front of him. Some best mate.

The noise of the crowd in the Ship's Inn Tavern sounded like a cacophony in Malcolm's head. He looked over at his bandmate, Angus Donaghue, who was laughing and celebrating his new relationship with Kerry Hunter. Those two had finally, after years of bickering, admitted they loved each other. He wouldn't ruin their night, but he needed some air. He stalked off toward the door, weaving through the crowd.

"Mack!"

Malcolm heard Brett calling after him but didn't turn around.

"Oy! What's up with Mack?" Angus yelled down the bar at Brett as he watched his friend stalk toward the door.

Brett just shook his head at Angus and mouthed "Later" over the noise.

Slamming at the heavy wooden door, Malcolm exited the pub and headed out into the darkness of the North Berwick night.

Malcolm shoved his hands in his pockets and continued up Harbor Terrace, trudging aimlessly ahead. The street was quiet since most people were in the pub, so all he had were his thoughts, and he had plenty of those. Some of which he wished he didn't. Fifteen years and just her name still felt like a broadsword slicing through his heart. That's why none of them ever said it. The guys knew that if they valued their life, her name was never to be mentioned. He managed to keep that pain, and the rest of his emotions, on ice most of the time. Like it or not, that was the only way to go on. Better to not feel anything than to feel that stabbing agony again. Ever. Between his mates now going all moony and falling in love and now this news, Mack wasn't sure he was going to be able to keep that up. Hearing her name just now chipped a huge crack in the ice block around his heart. He could feel that crack getting bigger with every step he took.

Bending Malcolm releases this summer! Stay tuned!

Where It All Began

Go back to the very beginning—Seeking Solace introduces readers to the world of The Captain's Folly men!

Bretton Keith sang the last notes of the popular ballad the pub crowd loved. He recognized everyone there as usual as he looked out from the small stage. The Ship's Inn Tavern was a local haunt and almost all of the patrons were villagers. Being less than an hour from Edinburgh, the town of North Berwick attracted enough tourism to boost the economy, yet it was small enough to remain fairly insular, especially on the harbor point. Most of the tourists tended to frequent the two or three higher-end establishments in town, and Bret liked that just fine. He prepped the boys for their last number of the set before break, a quick-paced Mumford & Sons cover. As they started the song, Bret saw the pub door open. Expecting to see a neighbor, Bret's eyebrows drew together for a moment as a lone stranger came in. Then, he lifted one eyebrow in appreciation of the attractive woman as she made her way to the bar and perched on a stool. Turning his attention back to the energetic pub crowd, he finished the song with a sly smirk on his face. Tonight, apparently, the monotony of village life just got a bit more interesting.

Twenty-four hours earlier...

Sarah Collier was in the bride's room waiting for the stylist to finish putting her long, dark auburn hair into an elaborate up-do. Sarah's four closest friends were chatting away behind her as they put the last touches on their makeup. The door to the hallway opened, and her mother, Sylvia, and sister, Elizabeth Collier Suitor, came through excitedly. As the stylist showered Sarah's head with a final blast of firm-hold hair spray, Sarah caught her mother's eye in the mirror.

"Sarah, darling! You are simply beautiful. I can't believe you're getting married today. Oh sweetheart!" Sylvia Collier rushed forward in a wave of lavender taffeta to embrace her youngest daughter. She leaned down and gave Sarah a sideways hug as the stylist stepped away to put her tools of the hair trade into a rolling suitcase.

Sarah smiled at her mother in the mirror and gave a self-deprecating chuckle. "I know, I know.

"Victoria and I have hoped for this since you and Darryl wer children."

As Sylvia spoke again, the bells of New London's First Con gregational Church began to peal from the steeple that rose hig above the church. The mother of the bride then turned to her old est daughter standing to the side. "Elizabeth! Is it six o'clock al ready!?"

"I think so. All the guests are seated, and the ushers have lit a the candles. The organist is ready when we are."

Sarah turned in her vanity chair and looked around the roo Her four bridesmaids were dressed in dark purple satin ball gow as was her sister. There was a glass table along the wall that he bouquets of lavender freesia and white roses with the end capped by a large trailing cascade of the same flowers mixed with English ivy which was to be hers. She saw Elizabeth standing by the door, smiling and giving Sarah a playful wink when their eyes met. Sarah automatically smiled at her sister, then turned back to the mirror. "Where's Lorraine? Shouldn't she be here now? I haven't seen her since she went to check on the groomsmen."

"I'll go see if I can catch her," offered Elizabeth, and she hurried from the room to locate the wedding planner.

While her mother crossed to the bridesmaids to make sure they were all ready for the ceremony, Sarah looked at her reflection in the large gilt mirror in front of her. Her lace covered wedding dress was off the shoulder, with a sweetheart neckline. She wore simple pearls in her ears and around her neck. Her auburn hair was twisted into loops and curls on top of her head, with a pearled accent clip on one side and a fingertip veil that fell from beneath the mass. Her face was flawlessly and delicately made up, and her brown eyes looked back at her from the mirror. She looked like a blushing bride, but did she feel like one?

The steeple bells had since stopped their ringing, and the old stone church sat in silence. The bridesmaids and Sylvia started to question what the delay was, and their eyes were darting from watches, to each other, to the clock on the wall. Sarah and the others had gathered in the center of the room, as the door burst open and Sarah's cell phone started chiming out the chorus to "Going to the Chapel". Hayden Collier barreled into the bride's room with Elizabeth and her husband, Brandon Suitor, rushing in behind him, and the missing wedding planner, Lorraine, trailing in last, clutching her clipboard for dear life.

"I'll kill him! What on earth is that boy thinking!" shouted Hayden, red-faced with outrage, the buttons on his tuxedo coat straining from his exaggerated huffing.

Of course, at this entrance, all the girls in the bride's room gasped and started demanding to know what was going on. Lorraine ran up to Sylvia, apologizing profusely and trying to stay in her good graces. In the middle of all the confusion and anger and dramatics, Elizabeth and Brandon walked over to Sarah. She had shifted away from the group upon her father's outburst, fearing and hoping what appeared to be happening.

"Sarah." Elizabeth came up and hugged her sister. "The groomsmen haven't seen Darryl since this morning, and his father has just told us that Darryl has sent word that he's not coming."

Sarah pulled away from her sister and stared back at Elizabeth and Brandon. Then, she remembered the cell phone going off. She crossed the room to reach the vanity table where she had been sitting. Retrieving her phone from the bag beside the table, she noticed she had a text message.

Darryl Morris's parents, Clyde and Victoria, entered the open door and walked over to the Colliers. "Hayden, you know how young men are. This will pass—boy's just having cold feet," Clyde Morris excused.

"We've had this planned since they were children, Morris! Cold feet? You can't tell me that you and Victoria are thrilled about this little development!" Hayden countered.

Sarah blocked out the noise around her as Sylvia and Victoria started getting hysterical about all their plans for their children's perfect future going to ruin. She could only focus on the message on her phone.

Darryl: Sarah—I just can't do this with you. I know the old men have been counting on this for years, but we wouldn't make each other happy. We both know we stayed in this out of loyalty to our parents and convenience sake. Besides, I think I want to see how things work out with Miranda. Sorry.

"Who's Miranda?" Sarah asked no one in particular, putting one hand on her hip, and the hand holding the phone dropping to her side. She stared in front of her, her face blank.

"What's that, sweetheart? Oh, my poor darling!" Sylvia rushed over to Sarah for another sideways embrace. Everyone stopped bickering and talking and focused on Sarah.

She stood stiffly with her mother's arms around her shoulders. *Breathe in, breathe out. Breathe in, breathe out. Blink.* Needing to move, she gently shrugged her mother's arms away and started to pace.

"I said," Sarah repeated more loudly and pointedly, "who is Miranda?"

"She's the girl Darryl's been seeing for a few months on the side," explained Darryl's cousin, college roommate, and best man, Aaron.

Everyone whirled around in shock at his statement. He hurriedly threw up his hands in defense. "Hey! Don't shoot the messenger!"

He looked Sarah in the eye through the small and distressed crowd of friends and relatives. "I thought you had a right to know since he's gone and jilted you."

Sarah's face shifted from surprise to suspicion, and Aaron quickly added, "Before you ask, I just found out last night during the bachelor party we had after the rehearsal. She works for one of the firms that Morris Investments does business with. He mentioned something about meeting her at a client luncheon. Apparently, he was very discreet...until now. "

"Months!" "What?" exclaimed both fathers at the same time.

A chorus of shouts, accusations, and lamentations erupted from the bridal party. Unseen by the others, Sarah walked out of the room. She looked back to see Lorraine jogging after her.

"Are the guests still sitting out there?" Sarah quietly asked.

Lorraine looked regretfully at the lovely bride in front of her. "Yes, we just found out all of this and haven't said anything yet. I know they're getting restless."

Sarah continued down the hall with Lorraine right behind her. She pulled on the large heavy door that opened into the side of the sanctuary. She could hear the buzz and hum of hundreds of people all talking at once, the creaking of wooden pews, scuffles of shoes over stone. Taking a deep breath, she entered the sanctuary and walked up the steps to meet the white-robed reverend, waiting behind the altar. She could hear the voices quiet, the hushed whispers of presumed disaster, surprised gasps, more creaking of pews as she crossed the carpeted pulpit. She asked the reverend if she could make a statement. He backed up a few paces, and she stepped into his place, the center of everyone's attention.

"Thank you all so very much for choosing to share what is supposed to be a special moment with us," Sarah began.

Inhaling, she panned over all the faces looking up at her in the candlelight. Friends, family, clients of the families' businesses, so cial acquaintances, strangers. She saw visions of white roses, purple freesia, and ivy in the periphery of her vision. She lifted her chin just the slightest bit. *Don't let them see your embarrassment. You've got to keep it together for a little while longer. Treat this like removing a Band-Aid—quick and brief.* She fought hard to push down a sudden wave of nausea.

"Unfortunately, Darryl won't be able to be here as well. I can assure you that he's well. Your presence here today is very appreciated by our families, but you won't need to stay." Exhaling, she turned from the congregation of guests and exited the pulpit through the open side door. The shocked echoes from the crowd followed her into the hallway, and she made her way back to the bride's room, clenching her fists against the rising anger. *It's not enough that I have to deal with being jilted at the altar. My entire family is so busy arguing about it, that I had to actually make the announcement. Talk about adding insult to injury!*

She entered the room to find Aaron gone, Brandon and Elizabeth sitting on a settee in the corner, her parents still arguing with the Morrises, and her bridesmaids gathering their things together. They all stopped as Sarah came in.

"I've informed the guests they don't need to stay. It's rude to keep them sitting out there with no explanation."

She reached up and removed the veil from her hair and tossed it onto her bouquet over on the glass table. Hayden walked over and patted her shoulder.

"That's my little trooper. We'll have this fixed in no time. Don't you worry, princess."

"You can't fix my son, Collier! He doesn't need fixing!" Clyde interjected.

"The hell he doesn't, Clyde!"

Sarah groaned in frustration. "Please! Just stop! Darryl has obviously made his choice, and there you have it. This isn't getting us anywhere or helping anything."

Sarah's gaze roved over the families. She started pulling the pins from her hair; she was getting a headache. "Can you all please go out there and tend to the guests and the reverend?"

"We can't leave you alone, honey!" Sylvia exclaimed and rushed forward.

"How can we help?"

"He's not worth it!"

"We're here for you, Sarah." All of her bridesmaids surrounded her in a group hug, affirming their support.

"Thank you. Please, I just need a few minutes to collect my thoughts. Besides, Mom, you want to minimize the social damage this will do..."

Sarah knew the way to clear everyone from this room. The threat of gossip or scandal was always the quickest. Everyone left reluctantly, and Sarah was finally alone in the large, beautiful room. She stared again at her reflection in the mirror. Her auburn hair was now hanging loose in waves around her shoulders. She ran her fingers through and linked her hands behind her head. She looked up at the ceiling, sighing loudly.

I'm supposed to be upset. Upset? No. Heart-broken? No. Embarrassed...yes. Furious...yes. They're going to come back soon and smother me with concern then ignore me while they fight about how this affects the family's plans. Get out... I have to get out of here...now.

Sarah reached behind her and yanked the zipper on her dress; it dropped to the floor, puddling at her feet. She ran across the room to the vanity where her bag was waiting. She had put in a traveling outfit for changing into after the reception. She quickly pulled on the black slacks and purple sweater and shoved her feet into black leather flats. She threw her phone into the bag and pulled out her car keys. She grabbed the bag and ran out to where her late-model Volvo was parked.

Naturally, her family had discovered her covert departure from the church shortly after she had hit the interstate. She could hear her cell phone chiming "Going to the Chapel" every few seconds with calls and text messages from her mother, father, sister, brother-in-law, and friends. *That stupid song! Elizabeth had to go and put that up there last night during the rehearsal dinner.*

One hour, thirty-five text messages, and seventeen missed calls later, she was standing at an airline check-in counter. After much deliberation with the attendant and an extra transfer fee of a couple hundred dollars, she managed to switch the tickets for tomorrow morning for the flight leaving in three hours. She checked her bags made her way through security. After what felt like the longest three hours of her life, Sarah finally boarded a plane heading far away from Connecticut. In the crowded cabin, her cellphone suddenly filled first class by once again pinging out the melody to "Going to the Chapel". Mid-phrase, the phone suddenly went silent.

Elizabeth: Sarah??!! Where are you? Everyone here is frantic! Please call someone!

Sarah glanced at the text message on her screen as well as the notification that she had now missed twenty-three phone calls. Muffling an exasperated sigh, she quickly powered down her phone and shoved it deeply into her large designer handbag.

Static poured from the overhead intercom. "Ladies and gentlemen, we're beginning our pre-flight check. Please make sure your seatbelts are secured and all electronic devices are turned off at this time." A brief pause was interrupted by more static. "This is Captain Andrew Shift. Looks like a great night for our flight. Cabin crew please prepare for takeoff. We should be landing in Edinburgh in approximately six and a half hours. Weather looks good from here, so it should be a smooth flight. Sit back and relax, folks. We're first in line for takeoff on runway 4-A."

In the seat across the aisle, an elegant, older lady leaned over and asked, "Is this your first time to Scotland?"

Sarah turned her head, offering a polite, yet cool, smile. "Yes, it is."

"Traveling by yourself, are you? How independent!"

Sarah laughed softly and hollowly. "Yes, independent."

"Are you going on a vacation or for work, dear?"

Sarah looked at the older woman for a long moment before answering solemnly, "I'm going on my honeymoon."

Want more? Find Seeking Solace on Amazon[1].

---

1. *http://a.co/dx7dMr3*

About the Author

Adrienne Dunning is simply a Southern gal who has fun playing poorly at golf when she's not crafting novels. She loves all forms of expression—writing, dancing, cooking, talking—and does them frequently and with abandon. She lives in coastal North Carolina and uses that region as the setting for many of her stories.

You can reach her on Facebook at www.facebook.com/adriennedwrites[1], on Twitter at @adriennedwrites, or by email at adriennedwrites@gmail.com. Visit her website at www.adriennedunning.com[2] for more information about upcoming releases and insightful blog posts about this crazy ride called "being an author".

1. http://www.facebook.com/adriennedwrites
2. http://www.adriennedunning.com

Made in the USA
Monee, IL
07 July 2021